A CRAZY MIXED-UP SPANGLISH DAY

GET READY FOR MORE GABÍ!

GET READY FOR GABÍ!

A CRAZY MIXED-UP SPANGLISH DAY

by Marisa Montes

illustrated by Joe Cepeda

> * That's Gabí. Not Gabi. As in Ga-BEE.
> With an accent. But not yet. And you're
> about to find out why!

A
LITTLE APPLE
PAPERBACK

SCHOLASTIC INC.
New York Toronto London Auckland Sydney
Mexico City New Delhi Hong Kong Buenos Aires

ISBN 0-439-47519-8
Text copyright © 2003 by Marisa Montes.
Illustrations copyright © 2003 by Scholastic Inc.
SCHOLASTIC, LITTLE APPLE, and associated logos are trademarks
and/or registered trademarks of Scholastic Inc.

12 11 10 9 8   5 6 7 8/0
                                                               40

Printed in the U.S.A.
First printing, April 2003

In loving memory of
my dear cousin "Miguelito"
Miguel Antonio Aponte Montes
July 22, 1947 – April 2, 2001
— M.M.

For Adriene
— J.C.

Acknowledgments

Special thanks to the third-grade teachers of Contra Costa Christian Schools in Walnut Creek, California, Sarah Gunst and Brian Huseland, for your time and patience. For all your insightful input, support, and encouragement, I'd like to thank Raquel Victoria Rodríguez, Susan Elya, Corrine Hawkins, Angie Williams. To third graders Ethan Williams and Janine Elya — you won't believe this! — a special BIG thanks for adding yet another dimension to Gabí.

Thanks to my family: Dr. Carmin Montes Cumming, my aunt, for being my Spanish consultant and being so enthusiastic about this project; my parents, Rubén and Mary Montes, for your constant love and belief in me; and my husband, David Plotkin, for all your love and support and computer expertise.

Thank you to my editor, Maria S. Barbo, for your wonderful ideas and suggestions, for brainstorming with me, and for your patience and flexibility in allowing me to write this book in my own style! And thanks especially to my agent, Barbara Kouts, for being a good friend and helping me be in the right place at the right time. Here's to good karma!   — M.M.

CONTENTS

UNO
CHAPTER 1
BOOT TROUBLE!

"Expecting trouble?" Mr. Fine's bushy eyebrows knitted into one long, fuzzy caterpillar.

He eyed my red cowgirl boots.

Red. My favorite color.

Papi says red is bold and sassy, like me.

Mami says I'm *un ají picante* — a hot chili pepper — which is also red.

And in case you were wondering, I'm Maritza Gabriela Morales Mercado.

At home, I'm Gabi. At school, I'm Maritza Morales. Mercado is Mami's last name, so I don't use it in school.

"Maritza? The boots?" Mr. Fine waited for an answer.

"Well . . ." I sat up straight. "I thought there may be some . . . problems today."

I craned my neck to glare at Johnny Wiley. He sits a couple of rows to my left and one row back.

Johnny was spiking up his hair.

Today is Crazy-hair Day. Once a year, we get to wear our hair in weird, wacky ways. It's fun. Somehow Mami had gotten my wavy brown hair into two high ponytail braids — one over each ear.

You could tell Johnny thought he was soooo cool. His dark blond hair was all spiked and sprayed blue and red on the ends. Boys LOVE Crazy-hair Day. Most of them looked like wacko space monsters.

Johnny mouthed something. I knew what it was.

My eyes scrunched up.

He mouthed the words again. I made an I'll-get-you-later face.

"Maritza?"

My eyes snapped back to Mr. F. I flashed him my best good-girl smile.

Mr. F's long caterpillar eyebrow split back into two. They bounced high above his glasses.

"We've talked about this before, Maritza. There are better ways to solve . . . problems . . . than with one's feet."

My shoulders slumped. I nodded. "Yes, Mr. Fine."

Mr. F is the nicest teacher I've ever had. But sometimes, I don't think he remembers being a kid.

I looked up at Mr. Fine. He's tall and thin so he had to bend down to look at me eye to eye. "Don't make me have to tell you again, Maritza."

"But —"

"No buts. If you even aim one boot at another student, I'll take them away and I won't give them back to you until the end of the day."

I sank down at my desk and tucked my boots as far under my seat as they'd reach.

My favorite uncle, Tío Julio, sent me these boots. They have tiny stars and curly

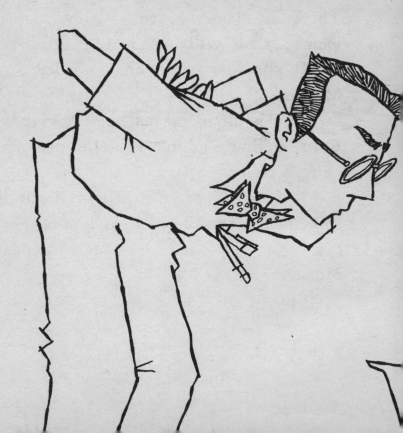

half-moons carved in the red leather and painted white.

Red and white: my favorite color combo.

Mr. Fine turned to the other students. "Okay, class. Take out a sheet of paper. As part of our new project, I want you to make a list of strange or interesting animals you'd like to learn about. Try not to choose common pets or farm animals."

Billy Wong asked, "What about Melvin?"

"Good question, Billy. An iguana is a very interesting animal."

Melvin is our class pet. Mr. F keeps him

in a big aquarium at the back of the room. We measured Melvin once. He's almost two feet long, if you count his striped tail.

There was a lot of mumbling. A few kids said, "Cool!"

I glanced at Johnny, moved one foot forward, and quietly tapped the toe of my boot.

I knew what I'd LIKE to write at the top of my list — the animal that looks most like Johnny Wiley: *Un sapo gigante* — a big, fat TOAD!

DOS
CHAPTER 2
"I HAVE THE FLY
BEHIND MY EAR!"

Mr. Fine kept talking. He was walking slowly up and down the rows of desks.

"For this month's project, we'll break up the class into groups of three," Mr. Fine said. "Can anyone tell me how many groups that would be?"

Mr. F likes to check our math skills whenever he has a chance. Luckily, I like math. Numbers come easily to me.

What doesn't come easily is spelling. All those letters and rules! "I" before "e" or "e" before "i"? As Mami says, *"¡Ay, ay, ay, ay, ayyyyy!"*

I raised my hand.

So did one of my best friends, Jasmine Lange.

She had sprayed the tips of her black curls hot pink for Crazy-hair Day. Jasmine crossed her eyes at me.

I swallowed a giggle. I'm really lucky my teacher lets her sit right next to me.

"Jasmine?"

"Since there are eighteen students in our class, that would be six groups of three, Mr. Fine."

"That's right, Jasmine, six groups."

I crossed my fingers. "Do we get to choose who's in our group, Mr. Fine?"

Oops! I forgot to raise my hand. So, real quick, I stuck it up in the air.

"Not this time, Maritza." Mr. F waved a sheet of paper. "I've already made that decision."

Groans filled the room.

"Quiet down, class." He used his I-mean-it voice. "In real life, you won't always get to be in a group or a team with your best friends. You need to get used to what it's like to work with all sorts of people."

I started to get a bad feeling about this. I raised my hand again.

"Yes, Maritza?"

"Umm — Mr. Fine," I began. "I think I have the fly behind my ear."

The class broke into giggles.

Then Johnny said, "A fly? Sure! Flies love pizza! Maritza Pizza gets flies! Do you get fleas, too?"

He started to scratch under his arms like an itchy monkey.

"HEY!" I bolted toward Johnny.

Before I got two steps, Mr. Fine blocked

my path. His eyebrows knitted into that long, fuzzy caterpillar again.

He pointed to my seat.

I sat down.

Mr. Fine turned to Johnny. "John, that will be enough!"

My cheeks sizzled.

I clenched my teeth, crossed my arms over my chest, and stared straight ahead.

I felt like I'd bitten into some of Mami's raw *ajo* — garlic. Steam whooshed out of my ears.

"What's this about a fly, Maritza?" Mr. Fine peered behind my ears. "I don't see anything."

More giggles from the class. One glance from Mr. F and they shushed.

Now my whole face burned. "It's what Mami says when I have a feeling something bad is going to happen to me. She says I must have the fly behind my ear."

Mr. Fine nodded. Slowly. "Oh . . . I see . . . it's an idiom. From Puerto Rico?"

I shrugged. I wasn't sure what that meant.

Mr. F turned to write on the chalkboard.

Then — you won't believe this! — Johnny Wiley started hopping up and down the aisle, doing his itchy monkey act. He was all bent over and scratching under his arms.

"Maritza Pizza has flies!" He whispered so Mr. F couldn't hear. "Maritza Pizza has fleas!"

A few kids laughed.

I glared at Johnny. He gave me his nasty Wiley smile and sat down — real quick, before Mr. Fine could see him.

Billy Wong, one of Johnny's buddies, gave him a high five — but it was under the desk, so I guess it was a low five.

I turned around to look at my other best friend, Devin Suzuki. She sits right behind me. We were both wearing our hair almost the same way for Crazy-hair Day. We sprayed the braids purple. You couldn't really see it on my hair, but the purple was super-bright on Devin's because it's a lighter brown than mine.

Devin tugged her right braid and winked. Our secret it's-okay sign. We signal with our hair whenever we know the other one is feeling bad.

It made me feel better right away.

I tugged my right braid back at her and gave her a half grin.

On the chalkboard, Mr. F wrote the word IDIOM.

"An *ih-dee-um*," he pronounced the word slowly. "It's an expression — something people from a place or country say a lot and it catches on. Like 'The early bird catches the worm.'"

He turned to the class. "Can anyone give me another example of an idiom?"

Devin raised her hand. "That kid has ants in his pants?"

Then Devin glared at Johnny. Johnny just gave her a creepy Wiley smile.

Mr. F didn't notice. "Good, Devin. Anyone else?"

I grinned at Devin and gave my right braid a double tug. That means "Cool! Good job!"

Devin smiled so big I could see her braces. Devin has metal braces on her two front teeth to fill in the gap between them.

She must be happy because she doesn't usually smile big enough to show her braces. She's very shy about them.

She's very shy about *everything*. Basically, Devin's a very shy kid.

Sissy Huffer, NOT a good friend, raised her hand. "She's as mad as a wet hen?" Sissy was looking right at me when she said that.

I just stared, like I had no idea what she meant.

"That's right, Sissy. Very good." Mr. F nodded.

Sissy gave me a snooty smile and shook her blond curls. Sissy doesn't do anything for Crazy-hair Day. She can't stand to mess up her perfect curls.

"Apparently in Puerto Rico," Mr. F continued, "when someone has a feeling something bad is going to happen, people say — what's the expression, Maritza?"

"You have the fly behind your ear." I grinned. "Want to hear it in Spanish?"

"Please." Mr. Fine bowed. He gave me the go-ahead sign with a swish of his arm.

"*Tienes la mosca detrás de la oreja.*"

Mr. Fine knew a little Spanish. He wrote the phrase on the board.

"Maybe we can share idioms from other countries during the school year."

Back at his desk, he picked up the sheet of paper he had earlier.

"Now, for the six groups of three," he said. "Group One: Billy Wong, Mike Patel, and Jasmine Lange. Group Two: Sissy Huffer, Johnny Wiley, and Maritza Morales. Group Three . . ."

My eyes bugged out. I didn't hear the rest.

Johnny Wiley AND Sissy Huffer?

In the same group?

With me?

Working together?

¡Caracoles! Yikes! I KNEW I had the fly behind my ear!

TRE∫
CHAPTER 3
DOUBLE TROUBLE

"¡*Ay, ay, ay!*" Devin stopped so fast, I bumped right into her.

It was recess and we'd just stepped out of the girls' room. We were playing follow the leader on the way to the playground to meet Jasmine. She always races to the monkey bars the moment the doors open.

Devin was the leader today.

She skipped. I skipped.

She stuck out her rear and did a hip-wiggle dance. I stuck out my rear and did a hip-wiggle dance.

She hopped on one foot. I hopped on one foot.

She stopped short. I bumped right into her.

"*¿Qué?*" I glanced around. "What?"

"*¡Mira!*" Devin pointed. I looked.

Devin likes to practice her Spanish with me. Her family lived in Panama for four years while her dad worked for an American company there. She speaks really good Spanish, and she doesn't want to forget it.

"Isn't that your Little Buddy, Cecilia?" Devin asked.

Each third grader gets to be a Big Buddy to a kindergartner. We help them with special projects during school.

I got Cecilia Sanchez because she just moved to California from Nicaragua. She didn't speak much English yet.

Little Cecilia was squatting next to a tree by the kindergarten play area. She looked like a scared kitty. Cecilia's hands covered her face.

17

She was crying buckets of tears, or as Mami would say — *lloraba a lágrima viva.*

We ran to the play area.

"¿Qué pasa, Ceci?" I asked her what was wrong.

The moment Ceci saw me, she wrapped her arms around my middle. She stuck her face in my chest and cried harder.

I held her tight. Ceci is even smaller than I was at her age.

It made me feel very big. And important.

I wondered if that was what Papi felt like when he held me.

"Tell me, Ceci," I said in Spanish. *"Dime."*

She mumbled something into my chest.

"Ceci . . ." I pulled her away from me. Gently.

She grabbed back on and buried her face in my chest.

I tried once more. *"Dime, Ceci. ¿Qué pasa?* Tell me. What's wrong?"

But every time I pulled her away, she snapped back like a rubber band.

"Shh, *cálmate, cálmate* . . . calm down . . ." I whispered nice things to her. Like Mami does to me when I wake up crying from a nightmare.

"Is there a problem, girls?" Ms. Snippett, the teacher on duty, walked up to us.

"No sé," I told her.

Ms. Snippett just stared, like she didn't get what I'd said.

Then I realized I was speaking Spanish to a non-Spanish-speaking teacher. I was so upset, I was crossing my brain wires.

My face turned the color of my boots.

There's only one thing I can't stand more than Johnny Wiley: And that's mixing up Spanish and English. I only do it when I'm super-stressed.

I'm *very* proud of how well I can speak both languages. And I don't like making mistakes. It's soooooo embarrassing!

I looked up. "I mean, I don't know."

"Why are you crying, dear?" Ms. Snippett asked Ceci.

I shook my head. *"No entiende* — I mean, she doesn't understand much *inglés* — uh, English."

"Oh. Well, ask her again. In Spanish."

So I did. *"¿Qué pasa, Ceci?"* I pulled her away so I could hear.

My T-shirt was all wet. From tears and . . . I tried not to think of what else. Ceci had goo running from her nose.

"Un muchacho malo . . ." Ceci said, really blubbering.

Ms. Snippett handed her a tissue to blow her nose. "What did she say?"

"Un muchacho malo . . ." I told her.

"Well, I heard *that,*" said Ms. Snippett. "But what does she *mean*?"

Uh-oh! My brain is really losing it, I thought. Devin gave me a worried smile.

"Something about 'a bad boy' . . ."

Before I could say anything else, Ms. Snippett took Ceci's hand. "Tell her I'm taking her to the office to get some water and to lie down."

"Okay . . ." I told Ceci what Ms. Snippett said. But I told her in English.

I sighed and told her again. This time in Spanish . . . *I hope.*

The moment Ms. Snippett took Ceci away, Johnny Wiley ran by.

After he passed us, he stopped and turned. With a big, nasty smirk, he waved. "Hey, Pizza Face! Hey, Metal Mouth!"

The moment he said "Metal Mouth," Devin's lips snapped over her braces. She looked ready to cry.

I bit my lip. My boots itched to kick him. I sprang forward.

Devin grabbed my arm. "No, Maritza, don't do it!"

"Hey, Pizza, catch any more flies

lately?" Johnny laughed. He could be soooo awful!

Billy Wong and a couple of Johnny's other buddies gathered around him.

Devin squeezed my arm harder and whispered warnings in Spanish.

Then Johnny spotted something behind us. His smirk widened.

Johnny nudged Billy and pointed. "Hey, there's that little crybaby again. She still blubbering?"

We turned.

You won't believe this! Johnny was pointing at Ceci.

I glared at him.

"That *sapo gigante*!" I said to Devin. "Now he's picking on little kids! Wait till I get him!"

"No, Maritza!" Devin cried. "You'll get detention . . . or worse. Remember what Mr. F said. He'll take away your boots!"

"I can't let him get away with that! I'd rather slurp slugs!"

I tried to pull away from Devin. But she wrapped both arms around me.

"Let go, Devin!"

Devin and I went back to yelling at each other in Spanish.

I tried to make her let go, but she wouldn't.

Johnny and his friends kept laughing.

Devin kept holding me.

My head was spinning.

"*¡Deja que te agarre!*" I yelled at Johnny.

"What's that?" he shouted back, grinning like a T-rex. "I don't speak-a the lingo, Pizza Face."

I felt like a bag of piping-hot microwave popcorn about to explode.

I did it again. I mixed up my Spanish and English.

And *this* time to Wiley the Smiley.

My toes curled in my boots.

Again I tried to yank away from Devin. But she stuck to me better than a sticker to a notebook.

I tried to drag her with me, but she was too heavy.

I stomped my boot. "Wait till I get you!" I yelled again.

This time in the right language . . . *I think*.

Johnny howled and punched the air with his fist. "Boys RULE, girls drool!"

He and Billy high-fived. Then they started hopping and scratching under their arms, all hunched over like itchy monkeys.

"Oh, yeah?" I yelled back. "Well . . . well . . . go chew monkey chow!"

CUATRO
CHAPTER 4
TROUBLE STRIKES AGAIN!

"Okay, class," Mr. Fine said once we'd all settled down after recess. "As I started to explain this morning, for this month's project we're going to work together in teams. Each team will choose a different animal to study. Remember, the animal should be strange or interesting."

Our desks were already pushed together into our new teams.

I'd never seen six groups of grumpier third-grade faces. Papi would call them *caras largas* — long faces. That's what they say in Argentina, where he's from. Mami would say they had faces as long as a *güiro*.

A *güiro* is a musical instrument. It's made from a long gourd that's dried and hollowed out. Then they carve slashes on the sides. You play it by scraping the slashes with a metal fork. It makes a *grrr-grrr, grrr-grrr* sound like my little brother when he needs a nap.

I think *güiros* are fun.

Working in teams with your worst enemies is NOT fun.

And Mr. Fine had a talent for grouping people with their worst enemies.

On the other hand, Mr. F looked *más contento que un perro con dos rabos* — happier than a dog with two tails.

Mr. Fine walked to

the board. He began to write as he spoke. "First, you'll work together to choose one or two animals from each team member's list — the lists you made this morning. Then you'll vote on which animal to use for your project.

"Finally, you'll present your animal to the class — as a *team*." He said the last word like he meant business. "You may write a report, perform a play, make a video, build a model, or do anything else the team chooses.

"All right. Go to it."

Everyone was quiet as we studied our own

lists. Finally, people started talking about what to write on the team's animal list.

Sissy wrinkled her nose. "Making lists reminds me of my mom's grocery lists, which reminds me of food. And thinking of food makes me hungry. I wish I had a snack."

"I know how you can get a snack, Sissy." Johnny gave me a wicked grin.

I pursed my lips, steeling myself for one of his nasty comments.

"How?" Sissy just HAD to ask.

"We have free food, right here in our own team," he said. "Just pick pepperoni and cheese right off Maritza Pizza!"

Billy Wong was sitting in the group next to us. He reached over and jabbed Johnny. "Free food from Maritza Pizza! Good one, Wiley!"

Johnny snickered, all happy with himself. "Hey, Maritza P—"

That did it! Before Johnny even finished the word, I was at his side.

I towered over him.

In my boots, I always feel as if I can tower over anybody. Even though I'm the smallest kid in the class.

I took my favorite position: fists on my hips, boots slightly apart, toes pointed out.

I stared at him. Hard. If I were Dragon-Ella with her laser gaze, Johnny would be crispy toast. But I'm Maritza Gabriela Morales Mercado and my secret weapon is my good old pair of red boots.

I stomped my right boot once.

Johnny's eyes opened wide. He leaned away from me.

Twice.

Johnny let out a tiny squeak.

I grinned. *He won't be calling me THAT again for a long, long time. I promise you.*

"This one's for my Little Buddy, Ceci!" I growled.

Just as I hauled back my boot to kick him in the shin, I heard Mr. Fine call my name.

I could tell from his voice that I just went from Guate-*mala* to Guate-*peor*.

That means from *bad* to *worse*.

Then, the next thing I knew, Mr. F was making me take off my boots.

I spent the rest of the day walking around in my white socks!

CINCO
CHAPTER 5
"I'D RATHER EAT BEES!"

After school that day, I stomped into my bedroom and kicked off my boots. One boot went flying onto the bed. The other one almost banged me on the head. I grabbed them and hid them deep in my closet.

I ripped off my grubby socks and stuffed them in the laundry basket. Way down, under other clothes. There, Mami wouldn't notice how filthy they were until she did the laundry.

By then, she'd probably know what happened, anyway.

When I turned around, I felt like the walls were staring at me.

Actually, they were.

My walls are covered with posters. Some are of my favorite superheroes. Others are of real-life heroines I read about in a book called *Brave Women in History* that Abuelita, my grandmother, sent me from Puerto Rico. Mami and I read one story every night until we finished it.

Annie Oakley stared out from an old poster. She posed next to her saddle after a performance in *Buffalo Bill's Wild West Show*. She was NOT smiling.

Even Iviahoca, my favorite Taino heroine, didn't look happy. You say her name like this: ee-veeyah-HOH-kah. "Taino" is tah-EE-noh. The Taino were the natives who lived in Puerto Rico and nearby islands when Christopher Columbus landed.

Mami told me that Iviahoca means "behold the mountain that reigns" in the Taino language. Iviahoca was a very brave woman. She even risked her life to save her son when he was captured by Spanish soldiers.

I couldn't find a big picture of Iviahoca, so last summer, I drew her with crayons on poster paper. She's standing on a cliff, watching Spanish ships sail into a bay in Puerto Rico.

On the same wall, the Latin-American superwoman Dragon-Ella frowned down at me from a huge poster. A dark green cape — like dragon wings — blew behind her. With her jaws clenched, fists on hips, legs apart (my favorite pose), she can take on anything.

When I was a little kid, I used to think I could grow up to be a superhero like Dragon-Ella. I thought that if I wished long enough and worked hard enough, I could get superpowers like hers.

Of course, I couldn't. Superheroes only

exist in the movies or on TV or in the comics. But I never gave up on wanting to fight crime.

Someday, I'm going to grow up to be the head of a secret government agency. And the president of the United States will call me on a special red phone.

I'll live a double life: Everyone will think I'm a karate and kick-boxing teacher. But I'll really be fighting crime under a secret identity.

I plopped onto the bed and looked at my walls. All my favorite heroines stared down at me.

I held out my hands.

"Well, what did you want me to do?" I asked them. "I couldn't let him get away with it!"

Thinking I was talking to him, Tippy, my black-and-white tomcat, jumped onto my bed. (My family says his name the Spanish way — TEE-pee. I like to pick names for my pets and toys that are easy to say in both languages.)

Tippy greeted me in his usual way.

First, he rubbed up against my leg, sweet as could be.

Next, he stomped over my bare feet.

It's such a silly thing to do, I always have to laugh — even on a yucky day like today.

"Come on, Tippy!" I scooped him up and swished him around. "You want to fly like Dragon-Ella?"

I landed Tippy on the bed next to me.

"You won't believe this, Tippy! Mr. Fine *me quitó las botas* — he took away my boots. He said I wasn't allowed to wear them to school ever again."

I always talk to Tippy in Spanish. That's all he speaks. Not like me or my family. We speak English *and* Span-ish. But at home, we *only* speak Spanish.

That's why Tippy doesn't understand anything else.

"I spent the afternoon walking around school in my socks. Mr. F only gave them back to me so I could walk home."

Tippy looked at me and slowly closed his big green eyes. Then he turned his head away. He couldn't be more bored.

"Tippy!" I wiggled the mattress to get his attention.

Tippy's eyes flew open. But when he saw it was just me, he closed them again.

I sat up and tickled my silly cat behind the ears. "*Esto es serio,* Tippy. This is serious! Mr. Fine made me promise never to wear my boots to school again. And to make

sure I won't forget, he wrote it in a note to Mami and Papi.

"They have to

sign the note, and I have to bring it back to school tomorrow. *¡Caracoles!*" I flopped back on the bed.

Tippy stretched and yawned. Then he lay on his side and got comfortable.

This time I had to smile.

I couldn't help it. I just remembered the look on Johnny's face.

"You know what, Tipito?" (Tipito means "Little Tippy.") "The look on Johnny Wiley's face and that little squeak he made when he thought I was going to kick him made it all worth it."

Tippy started purring. His eyes were closed. His lips curled up in a kitty smile. The black spot on his chin wiggled like he was laughing.

"Miaouu . . ." he said softly.

"I knew you'd understand!" I hopped up so I was standing on the mattress. "You wouldn't have let old Wiley the Smiley get away with that nasty comment, either, would you, Tipito? Well, I didn't."

I started jumping on the bed.

"Nope!" I jumped. *"¡Claro que no!* No way!" I jumped higher. "I'd rather eat bees!"

I jumped so high and so hard, Tippy went flying. He landed on my rug and flicked his tail at me in a huff.

Then I noticed the heroines on my walls. They didn't seem as grumpy now.

"Come on, Tipito." I hopped off the bed and picked him up.

He squirmed a little. Then he licked my nose with his warm, sandpaper tongue.

I giggled. "Now, to make sure Mami and Papi don't take away my boots, too."

SEIS
CHAPTER 6
"WHEN THE FROG GROWS HAIR!"

"Gabi! Gabi! Gabi!"

A few minutes later, Miguelito, my four-year-old brother, came bouncing into my room. He just figured out I was home.

Like my parents, Miguelito always calls me by my middle name. When I was little, I couldn't say "Maritza Gabriela." But I could say "Gabi," short for "Gabriela." So Mami and Papi started calling me Gabi, too.

I was lying on my bed again. I groaned and rolled over.

Maybe he'll think I'm asleep . . .

"Gabi!" He yelled in my ear. His voice was as loud as a car horn.

. . . Or maybe not.

My ear was ringing. I grabbed my pillow and covered my head.

Miguelito was still yelling and bouncing next to me.

I dragged the pillow from my face.

"*Cuchichea*," I told him softly. "If you want to get someone's attention, whisper, okay?"

Mami did this to me when I was little, and it worked. It's amazing! She always made me listen by just speaking softly.

Maybe it would work with Miguelito . . .

He leaned over and whispered in my ear. "Gabi, guess what?"

"What?" I whispered back.

"MAMI AND PAPI HAVE A SECRET!"

. . . Or maybe not.

I grinned. If anybody stops talking when

Miguelito walks in on them, he thinks they have a secret.

Miguelito likes to blab everything he hears, so Mami and Papi don't talk about grown-up stuff when he's around. The moment he bounces into the room, they change the subject or stop talking.

But . . . you never know . . .

I sat up, ready to hear his big "secret."

"¿De veras?" I tried whispering again. "Really? How do you know?"

"Because they said something about —" He stopped.

I waited. His lips were pressed together. His eyes were as big as *platos* — plates. He was turning purple.

"*¡Respira!*" I said, giving his shoulder a little shake. "Breathe!"

Miguelito let out a big breath. He leaned in close. "*¡Una sorpresa!*" he whispered in my ear.

"A surprise?" I jumped up. Now *this* was something. "Are you sure?"

He nodded so hard his teeth rattled. And his dark hair flopped up and down.

"A surprise . . ." I repeated. "Hmm . . . Maybe I can snoop around after dinner."

"Can I snoop, too?" Miguelito started bouncing on his toes, letting his arms hang loose and limp. He looked like a floppy rubber doll on a string.

If I didn't answer soon, he'd let his jaw go all loosey-goosey. Then he'd moan, "Ahh-hhhhh," while he bounced and jiggled. So it would sound all jittery and jerky. He loved to do that.

He's such a goofball . . . but so am I!

I joined him, and we both bounced and jiggled and went, "Ahh-hhhh-hhh!"

"Soo-oo-oo, caa-aan III-eee snoo-ooop, too-oo?" he asked.

"Ooh-kaaaa-aaay," I answered.

Then I stopped and pressed a finger against my lips.

"But only if you're very, very *quiet*," I whispered. "Shhh . . ."

"Shhhh . . ." he whispered back.

Oh yeah, he'll be quiet, all right . . .

¡Cuando la rana eche pelo! — as Mami says. When the frog grows hair!

SIETE
CHAPTER 7
SPUNKY FEET

Fifteen minutes later, Miguelito was still jumping around my room. I needed to study for my spelling test, but he was NOT being quiet the way he'd promised.

"Miguelito," I said, grinning, "you'll be quiet *cuando la rana eche pelo,* won't you?"

Miguelito nodded and laughed extra loud. "HA! A froggie with hair!"

"*Shhh* . . . Think about it, Miguelito. Where would it grow? Between his toes?" I wiggled my bare toes. "Hairy frog webs!"

"Hairy webs! That would tickle!" He rolled on the carpet and laughed and laughed.

"Here," I said. "Show me how a froggie hops."

He crouched down and started hopping like a frog.

"That's right," I said, guiding him to the door. "Hop out to the family room for a while."

Miguelito's dark hair flip-flopped as he hopped. He'd make a good hairy frog.

Right then, Papi peeked in. When he saw Miguelito frog-hopping, he got down and started hopping, too. Then I got down. Now we were three hopping frogs.

Papi pooped out first and fell back on the carpet. I lay down next to him.

Miguelito bounced off to watch TV.

"How was your day, Gabita?" Papi asked when we were alone. He likes to call me "Little Gabi."

Papi tugged one of my ponytail braids. Then he kissed the top of my head.

I groaned and dragged myself to my desk. "Pretty yucky."

Papi pulled up a stool and sat next to me.

He nodded. "I had a pretty yucky day, too. One of my experiments blew up on me."

I checked him over. "No kidding. You forgot to take off your icky lab coat again."

Papi looked down at his lab coat. He nodded sadly. "*Es verdad*. So I did."

I like to think of Papi as a mad scientist. But the truth is that he's more like an absent-minded professor — like the one in that Disney movie. When he's working, he forgets about everything else.

Papi put his arm around me. "*Dime, Gabita*. Tell me what was so terrible about your day?"

I sighed and pulled Mr. F's note from under my book. "I can explain. I really can."

I told him about the whole awful day. As I talked, Papi's long, sad face got longer and sadder. He reminded me of a sad-eyed hound dog with droopy cheeks.

¡Pobre Papi! I'd made him feel bad.

Slowly, I handed him the note.

"Now Mr. Fine won't let me wear my boots to school. Will you sign this so Mami doesn't have to see it?"

He read the note. "You're going to have to tell her, Gabi."

"Why? We can tell her later —"

"No. Mr. Fine wants us both to sign," he said. "Anyway, we do not keep secrets from your *mami*."

I sighed. I was hoping that after a day or so, Papi would forget.

I gave it one more try. "But Mami gets so upset when I get in trouble!"

Papi shook his head sadly. "She worries about you. So do I. Gabita, you must try to control your spunky feet."

I giggled. "I have spunky feet?"

Papi nodded. He bit his lower lip, trying to look serious. "Afraid so."

But his green eyes were laughing.

"Oh, Papi," I said, already starting to feel better, "you're such a big silly."

"No, you're the silly." Papi faced me in his chair, ready to play the game we've been playing since I was little.

"No, *you're* the silly." I leaned in closer. *"Papi bobo."*

"No, *you're* the silly." Papi leaned in even closer. *"Gabita bobita."*

"No, you're the —"

"¡Topi!" And that's when Papi bumped my forehead with his. "I got you!"

"¡Ay, Papi!" I said, grinning really big. *"¡Cuánto te quiero!"*

"I love you very much, too, Gabita." Papi kissed my forehead.

"Now," he said, sitting back, "we have to talk about how to solve problems . . . *without* the use of spunky feet."

OCHO
CHAPTER 8
MY SECRET IDENTITY

Papi and I moved to my bed where he could sit next to me.

"Gabita, your *mami* and I worry about your temper." He put his arm around my shoulders.

"But, Papi," I said, "Johnny makes me see red."

"I thought you liked red."

"I like red, not *Johnny*!" I said his name with my upper lip curled up — the way I say *booger*.

"Anyway, my job is to fight evil. And

Johnny Wiley is one of the great evils of the universe!" I stared at Papi. "He's my worst enemy! The way El Bandido is Dragon-Ella's worst enemy."

I waited for Papi to act like a grown-up and tell me that I'm too young to have "a job."

He didn't.

Instead, he said, "I can understand that. You do your job the best way you know how. But part of having a job is learning new ways to do it better."

"It is?" I sat up straight. This sounded interesting.

"Oh, absolutely. People who are very good at their jobs are good because they keep trying to get even better. That's why they call what your *mami* does '*practicing* law.'"

Papi pulled me close. "Me, too. I have to

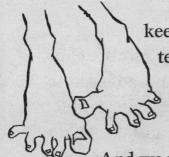

keep studying to become a better chemist."

I looked up. "But you're already so good!"

"We want to *stay* good. And we want to get *better*."

I thought about that. It made sense.

"So what should I do to be a better crime fighter?"

Papi scratched his cheek. "Well . . . might I suggest using your head, not your feet?"

My shoulders slumped. "No feet? But . . . they're my secret weapon — like Dragon-Ella's laser eyes."

"Superheroes only use their secret weapons when they have to. Look" — Papi took my hand — "doesn't Dragon-Ella lead a double life? And doesn't she do everything she can to protect her secret identity?"

"*¡Pues claro!* Of course she does!" I said. "Dragon-Ella is a firefighter. She can't let anyone know about her secret powers!"

"Why not?"

I rolled my eyes. Grown-ups sure are clueless sometimes. "Because she has to blend in with everyone else. Then the villains will let down their guards and make a mistake. That's how she finds out who the real bad guys are."

Papi nodded. "What would happen if she used her superpowers when she was fighting fires?"

"Papi!" I couldn't believe he had to ask. "Her cover would be blown. Then she couldn't catch the villains in the act and spoil their evil plans."

Papi smiled.

"Oh," I said, feeling a little silly I didn't catch on sooner. "I get it. I have to stop using my secret weapon at school. And I can't let on about my crime-fighting identity. My cover is third-grade student."

Papi kissed my forehead. "And a very good cover it is. Could even fool me. And I know the truth."

"But you're the only one."
I winked. "Let's keep it
that way, okay?"

Papi smiled. "You've
always dreamed of fighting
crime, Gabita. I'm so proud of
you for that. You're never too
young to start living your dream.
But remember, you'll have to start
learning to use this" — Papi tapped
my forehead — "instead of these."
He pointed to my bare feet. "And
you have to pretend you're a
regular kid."

"But we know different,
don't we, Papi?"

"That's right, super-*hija*.
We know different."

I grinned and gave Papi
a great-big, super-daughter hug.

NUEVE
CHAPTER 9
"BURGERS, ANYONE?"

"Mami, pasa las french fries, *por favor,"* I said to Mami at dinner that night.

Papi and I wanted Mami to be in a good mood when she heard about Mr. F's note. So he and I made dinner: hamburgers with our secret sauce, fries, and Mami's favorite avocado salad with lime-and-garlic dressing.

"Gabi, please don't mix your Spanish with English. If you want the fries, say it in Spanish." Mami is very strict about Miguelito and I speaking good Spanish at home.

Miguelito slurped his milk — real loud — and almost spilled it.

While Mami fussed with him, I thought for a minute. "Um . . . I think I forgot how to say 'french fries.'"

"See what happens when you get lazy and use the English word when there's a perfectly good Spanish word? You forget the correct Spanish word." Mami passed the fries, and at the same time she said, *"Papas fritas."*

"Oh," I said, "that's right. *Papas fritas.*" The last thing I wanted right now was to get Mami mad at me.

I glanced at Papi. He winked.

I bit into my hamburger. "Ummm, *muy bueno,* Papi. Very yummy."

Miguelito swung his legs as he munched on his burger. *"¡Sí, Papi, muy bueno!* Um-ummm! Yummy!"

"Mami, how do you like your —?" I gulped, almost choking on my burger.

I just realized I didn't know how to say "hamburger" in Spanish.

"*¿Cómo?*" Mami said. "What?"

"Uh . . ." My brain was racing. "Ham" is "*jamón*" in Spanish, but what is "burger"?

"Uh . . ." I tried again. "How do you like your *jamón-burgera?*"

Papi really did choke on his burger. He laughed and laughed and laughed.

Even Mami chuckled. "I think you mean *hamburguesa*, Gabi. But that was a very good try!"

"Ummm!" said Miguelito. "*Jamón-burgera!*"

His legs swung happily under the table as he took another big bite.

This time, everyone laughed.

After dinner, Papi asked, "Anyone ready for dessert?"

"*YAAAY!*" Miguelito clapped and swung his legs.

I clapped, too.

Then Miguelito and I started banging our spoons on the table. "*¡Helado! ¡Helado! ¡Helado!*"

I knew Papi had made his special *helado de coco* — coconut ice cream. We all love it.

Papi's timing was perfect.

Mami had on her grumpy *güiro* face. During dinner, Papi had told her about Mr. F's note. She was *not* happy.

Neither was I. I had a *cara larga*, too. I wondered if Mr. F's note had spoiled their surprise — whatever it was.

So I hopped up, glad to have something

fun to do. "Let me help, Papi! I'll get the *helado* from the *friser* —"

I shot a look at Mami. Her eyebrows flew up under her light brown curls.

Friser is Spanglish for "freezer" or "fridge." Mami hates when I use Spanglish.

Spanglish is when you take an English word and add some Spanish to it. Or when you say an English word with a Spanish accent, like *friser*. It sounds like it's really Spanish, but it's not.

"I mean *congelador*," I said.

"Maybe we should save it," Mami said. "Until after . . ." She gave Papi a funny look.

"Until after what, Mami?" Miguelito wiggled and bopped in his chair.

"Uh . . . after . . . I have a little talk with Maritza Gabriela," she said.

Uh-oh. Mami only calls me Maritza Gabriela when I'm in trouble. I had the feeling our talk wasn't going to be so "little."

DIEZ
CHAPTER 10
"SURPRISE!"

"Gabi! Gabi! Gabi!"

As Mami and I walked into the living room for our "little" talk, Miguelito ran in.

"*¡Una guagua! ¡Una guagua!*"

He was bouncing like he had springs on his feet and pointing toward the driveway. He kept screeching, "*¡Una guagua! ¡Una guagua!*" again and again.

My eardrums hurt. "A bus?" I covered my ears. "Out front?"

Miguelito nodded like crazy and tugged Mami and me by the arms to the living room window. Papi followed close behind.

In our driveway sat the airport van that picks up Mami for business trips. As we watched, the driver slid the side door open. He helped down a tall, thin lady with dark hair all rolled up in the back.

She looked kind of familiar.

I squinted. And — you won't believe this! — it was Abuelita! My grandma. Mami's mother. I hadn't seen her in a whole year.

Right behind her were Mami's brother and sister — Tío Julio and Tití Alicia!

"*¡Sorpresa!*" they yelled the moment they opened the front door. "Surprise!"

"YAAAY!" Miguelito and I shrieked.

I was so happy to see Abuelita, I practically ran down Mami and Papi getting to her.

Tío Julio flies in for business every few months. He just shows up and surprises us. Like now.

Tití Alicia lives only a few hours away so she visits a lot, too.

But we only get to see Abuelita once a year!

She scooped me up in her arms the way she used to when I was little. She's skinny, but strong. I didn't care that I'm too big to be held like Miguelito. It felt good.

"*¡Oo-iii!* Gabita, you've gotten so big!" Abuelita gave me a big kiss and hugged me tight.

I hugged her, too, and buried my face in her soft hair. It still smelled like I remembered. She calls it *lavanda* — lavender. It's a flower.

Tío Julio was holding Miguelito upside down and tickling his tummy. Miguelito was shrieking. "¡*No, no, Tío Julio! ¡No me haga cosquillas!* Don't tickle!"

Tío Julio made a face. "¡*Ay!* My ears! You've got a strong pair of lungs, Miguelito!"

Everyone else was hugging and kissing and laughing and talking at the same time.

Lots of loud Spanish. Lots of hands flying while talking. Abuelita finally had to put me down, so she could talk with her hands free. Nobody could hear what the other person was saying, but that didn't matter. That's the way it always is when Mami's family gets together.

While the grown-ups were all huddled up, Miguelito and I started a conga line around them. I was in the front and Miguelito was behind me, hanging on to my waist.

He and I sang: "La-la, la-la — ooo, ah!" all the way into the family room.

Then things got even louder.

"*¡Tío!¡Tío!¡Tío!*" Miguelito swung on Tío Julio's arm, trying to get his attention again. But Tío was talking to Papi about where to put all the bags.

I wanted Abuelita to know how much I liked *Brave Women in History*. I ran to my room to get it and waved it in the air.

"Abuelita! Abuelita, *¡Mira, mira!* The book you sent. I looove it!"

Mami, Abuelita, and Tití Alicia smiled and nodded at me, but everyone kept talking. I knew thcy heard me, though.

At last, Tío Julio and Papi took Miguelito to help carry the bags upstairs.

When things got quiet, we all sat on the couch. I snuggled between Tití Alicia and Abuelita.

Abuelita told us how Tío Julio came up with the idea to surprise us. "Julio paid me one of his famous surprise visits for my birthday. His present was this trip to California — so we could all be together."

She turned to me and stroked my face. "I'm so glad I'm here. You and Miguelito are growing up so fast! If it weren't for the pictures your *mami* sends, I'd hardly recognize you."

I hugged her.

I was glad she noticed how much I had grown in a year. Sometimes she still sends me babyish toys and clothes. But Mami and I didn't want to tell her and hurt her feelings. Maybe now she'll choose better presents. Like the book.

I looked into her eyes. It was like looking in a mirror. Abuelita has the same color eyes that I do. Gray-green with yellow speckles. It's called hazel.

But she has straight hair like Tití's, and I

have wavy hair. I've always wanted straight hair like theirs. Mami says mine has "body," and I'll like that when I grow up. But some mornings, my hair has so *much* body, I'm afraid it will walk off on its own!

Right then, Papi walked in carrying a tray with his *helado de coco*. He had drizzled it with *dulce de leche* — a type of caramel.

Tío Julio followed with a pot of coffee and cups.

Behind them, Miguelito balanced a bunch of spoons on a stack of napkins.

"*¡Rápido, rápido!* Quick, quick!" Miguelito said when he made it safely to the table. "*¡A comer!* Let's eat!"

Papi turned to Mami and winked. That's when I realized that Mami and Papi knew about Tío Julio's surprise visit all along. That's why Mami wanted to save the dessert for later. *That* was the surprise Miguelito heard them talking about.

The surprise for us kids!

ONCE
CHAPTER 11
A VERY ROUGH NIGHT

After dessert, we talked and talked and talked. Practically the whole night.

Miguelito fell asleep way before anyone noticed it was long past our bedtimes. So Papi took him up to his room. I made sure to be very quiet. I wanted to stay up and hear more stories about Puerto Rico, but Mami made me go to bed, too.

Even though it was very late, I couldn't sleep. I was so excited about Abuelita's visit. And I could still hear the rest of the family talking and laughing in the living room.

I could listen to them tell stories all night, if they'd let me.

Hmmm . . .

I crept out of bed and through the hallway. When no one was looking, I crawled under the dining room table and hid. Then Abuelita told a really funny story about Mami when she was little, and I laughed out loud.

That's when Mami caught me.

"Come on," she said, grinning, "off to bed. I'll tuck you in."

Once I was in bed, she sat next to me. "Gabita, always remember. No matter how angry your *papi* and I get, we'll always love you."

Then Mami gave me a big hug and kissed me good night. "Sleep well, *mi amor.*"

Still, I couldn't get to sleep. I tossed and turned and kicked the sheets off.

My brain was busy thinking: About Abuelita's surprise visit. About what Mami and Papi said. And about working with Sissy and Johnny for a whole month.

What if Johnny kept bothering me? What if all his teasing kept making me mad? Like it did on the playground with Ceci. And when I got my boots taken away.

I didn't want to think about that anymore. I was tired. I needed to get to sleep. . . .

I rolled over and turned on the radio. Maybe some music would help.

"Good night, Tipito." Tippy was snuggled on my window seat.

"*Miaouu.*" Tippy stretched and flopped over on his side.

"*Hasta mañana,*" I told him. "Until tomorrow . . ."

As I closed my eyes, loud Spanish voices mixed with the English words in the songs. The words got all smushed up in my brain.

The next thing I knew, a train was chugging through my bedroom.

"*RRRRR-rrrr . . . Ahhhhhh! RRRR-rrr-rrr-rr . . . Aahhhhh!*"

No . . . not a train . . . something else . . . something close by . . .

Something loud and raspy and right next to me.

Something was in bed with me!

I bolted up. I was breathing hard. My heart was pounding like bongo drums.

Then I smelled it — lavender.

"Oh, *gracias* — thank you!" I lay back down. "It's just Abuelita."

I forgot she was going to sleep with me. Tití Alicia was using the guest room. Tío Julio was in Miguelito's room. Abuelita would move to the guest room when Tití left.

She must have turned off the radio because all I could hear was "*RRRRR-rrrr . . . Ahhhhhh! . . .*"

¡Caracoles! I thought. Can you believe it? *¡Abuelita ronca!* She snores! And LOUD, too!

I tried putting my pillow over my head.

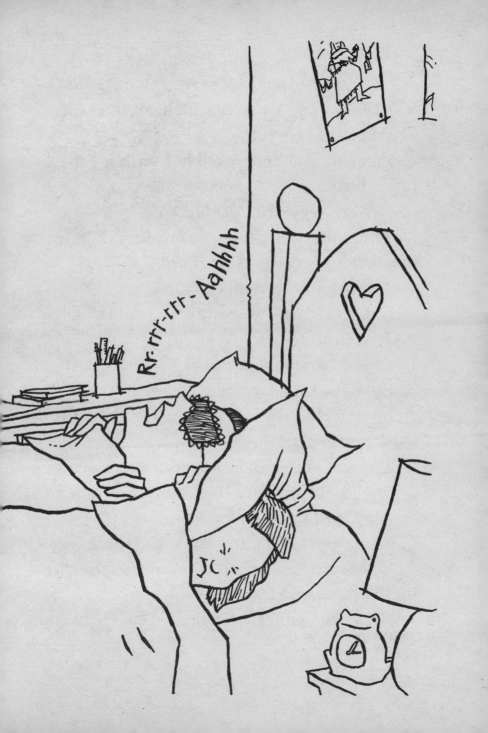

"Rr-rrr . . . Aaahh! Rr-rrr-rrr . . . Aahh!"

¡Ay, ay, ay! I could still hear her. But now I couldn't breathe.

I reached out and poked her with my toe. Just a little.

"Rr-rrr-rrr-rrr . . . Aahhhhh!"

Then she rolled over. Toward me. She took a deep breath. *"Aahhhhh!"*

After that, she stopped snoring.

But now that I was awake, I couldn't get back to sleep.

I tossed and turned.

I watched my froggie clock with the big green hands in his belly tick away the minutes. It was 2:05!

The rest of the night, when Abuelita was quiet, I slept a little. But then she'd start snoring, and I'd wake up again.

So most of the night, I lay in bed thinking.

I thought about all the mean things Johnny does and says to people.

He picked on little Ceci.

He called Devin "Metal Mouth."

And he called me Maritza Pizza and made me so mad I lost it and got my boots taken away. I even yelled at him in Spanish.

But soon, Ceci will get bigger, and he'll stop picking on her.

And next year, Devin's braces come off. Then he can't call her "Metal Mouth" anymore.

But I won't change. *I'll always be Maritza Pizza. . . .*

A car passed on the street. Its headlights lit up my wall.

I spotted my picture of Annie Oakley.

. . . Or will I?

I'd just thought of a perfect plan!

A perfect way to fix my worst enemy's evil ways!

DOCE
CHAPTER 12
A CRAZY MORNING

Way before I was ready the next morning, my froggie alarm began to croak: *"Rib-bit! Rib-bit! Rib-bit!"*

I rolled over and slapped the OFF button on his head.

Then my backup alarm came on: My radio blasted the D.J.'s voice in English.

And that's when the door banged open.

"¡Levántate! Get up! Get up! Get up!"

Miguelito bounced beside my bed, shaking me. He kept shrieking in Spanish. His loud shrieks hurt my ears. And the radio blared away in English.

Abuelita poked her head in and said something in Spanish about breakfast. Then she rushed back out.

"¡*Ayyyyyyy!*" I slid out of bed and Miguelito hopped on my bare foot. "¡*Wáchate, Miguelito!*"

¿*Wáchate? Is that even a word?* I think I meant to say "watch out."

I put my hand on his arm and tried again. "Miguelito, *shhh. ¡Cálmate!* Calm down!"

I stumbled to my closet. I pushed aside all the piles on the floor and found my boots.

I slipped them on. They're always the first thing I put on in the morning. I think better with my boots on.

And right then, I really needed them because my head was all fuzzy-feeling and full of cotton.

I scooted Miguelito out the door, promising to play with him after school.

Then I stomped across the floor. Back and forth, back and forth. Picking out my clothes. Brushing the body out of my hair. Looking for the bathroom . . .

¡Ay, ay, ayyyyyy! The spelling test! I still had to look over my spelling words. I forgot to study them last night.

As I stumbled toward the kitchen, Tío Julio's booming voice yelled over everyone else's: "*¡Caramba!* It sounds like *un gallinero* in here!"

Un gallinero is a chicken coop. But it also means a "loony bin." Knowing Tío Julio, he probably meant the second one.

"So, Julio, does that make you *el gallo guapo*?" Tití Alicia loves to tease her brother.

Tío Julio began to strut around, flapping his elbows like a handsome rooster. Tití Alicia followed him, bobbing her head like a chicken.

Everybody laughed — even me. The kitchen sounded like three *gallineros* in one!

Then Miguelito clucked to the TV and turned up the volume. He was watching *Sesame Street*.

Now I had Spanish going in one ear and English going in the other.

"*¡Gabrielita, ven a comer!*" Abuelita had cooked breakfast and wanted me to come eat it. She put a *tortilla de guineo* on the table.

"*Tortilla de* banana, my favorite!"

I did a little hop-skip-wiggle dance in place and skipped to the table. Mami eyed my feet. She raised one eyebrow and crossed her arms. No one else noticed. They kept talking.

I looked down
at my feet.

Oops! My boots. I
forgot I wasn't allowed to
wear them to school.

I raced back to my room
and kicked them off. This
time one boot did bang me

on the head. *"Ow!"* I rubbed my head, and quick as a gecko, slid into my sneakers.

Just as I ran out of my room, I remembered Mr. Fine's note. I rushed back to grab it.

Back in the kitchen, I tried to enjoy my banana omelet, but my eyelids kept drooping.

Next thing I knew, Tío Julio was pulling my plate from under my face and raising my head off the table.

I couldn't believe it! I fell asleep in my *tortilla!* ¡*Caracoles!* Did *I* have egg on *my* face!

I glanced at the clock. Oh, no! I was soooo late! And Papi had just left, so I couldn't get a ride with him.

I wiped my face, kissed everyone good-bye, grabbed my stuff, and raced for the door.

Halfway down the block, I remembered my lunch. I raced back home. I banged open the front door, ran for the kitchen, and tripped on the carpet. I went flying and slid across the kitchen floor on my belly.

"*¡Gabi!*" everyone screamed at the same time.

"*¿Gabi, qué pasó?*" Mami and Tío Julio rushed to my side. Tío helped me up.

"*Estoy* okay," I said. "I just tripped *en la . . . carpeta*. I forgot *mi,* uh . . . *lonche,* so I ran back . . ."

Mami checked me over and made sure I was really okay. Then she asked, "Gabi, why are you speaking Spanglish? You know that *carpeta* and *lonche* are not really Spanish words."

I blinked. I hadn't even noticed.

"I . . . uh, I tripped *en la alfombra,*" I said — the right way. *I hope.* "I forgot *mi almuerzo,* so . . ."

Abuelita grabbed my lunch bag and brought it to me. "Leave the child alone, Isa. Can't you see she's upset because she's late? Go on, Gabrielita, run along."

Abuelita walked me to the door and hugged me good-bye.

Luckily, Devin and Jasmine were still waiting at our morning meeting spot.

Jasmine took one look at me, looked down at herself, and crossed her eyes. "Did I miss an announcement?" she asked. "Is today 'Backwards Day'?"

As usual, Jasmine was perfectly dressed in a cute top with purple glitter beads and matching pants.

For the first time since I got dressed, I looked down at myself. I had on wrinkled jeans, no socks, and — you won't believe this! — the inside label on the back of my top was tickling my chin.

My shirt was on inside out and backwards!

Devin gave me a silly crooked smile —
like she wanted to laugh, but didn't want to
hurt my feelings.

"*¿Qué pasó?*" Devin glanced at Jasmine
and repeated in English. "What happened?"

I started to tell her in English — so
Jasmine could understand — but the words
kept coming out all funny. I was speaking
half English and half Spanish.

"Hey, no fair!" said Jasmine. "You guys

promised not to speak Spanish when I'm around. You know I can't understand it!"

We were late, so we started walking. Fast.

I tried telling them again. "*Mi abuelita* — my grandmother — *llegó* . . . uh . . . got here *anoche* — um, last night — and so did my *tío* and *tití*. We stayed up practically *toda la noche* talking.

"Then Abuelita *roncó, Rrrr-rrrr-rrrr* . . . *Ahhhh! Rrr-r-rrrr* . . . *Aaahhh!* All night! So *me desperté,* and when I was *comiendo mi tortilla, me dormí* — I, um, fell asleep — in my eggs!"

We were almost running. I started to get a stitch in my side from walking and talking so fast.

"And the *keechena* — um, *cocina* — kitchen — was like a chicken bin — I mean, a loony coop — no, no, a loony bin! With Spanish in one ear, and *inglés* in the other . . ."

When I finished my story, I turned to Jasmine. "Jasmine?"

She wasn't there. I looked back.

She was standing on the sidewalk. Staring at us. Her mouth was hanging open.

Devin and I stopped, too. When Jasmine saw us looking, the corners of her mouth turned down. She seemed ready to cry.

Oh, no! I thought. *I've hurt her feelings.*

I shook my head. What was happening? Everything was going wrong.

I felt like those silly cartoon characters that get bonged on the head. When they wake up, they don't even know where they are.

I grabbed Devin's arm and we ran back to Jasmine.

"*Lo siento* — I mean, I'm sorry, Jasmine!" I told her. "Really! I didn't mean to make you feel left out. *No dormí* — I, uh . . . didn't get enough sleep last night. Now my tongue is all twisted!"

Jasmine blinked. She looked at me and turned to Devin. Devin shrugged.

Then — good old Jasmine! — she gave me a goofy grin. And crossed her eyes.

"Let's hurry and get to school." She pointed at the label under my chin. "You need to get to the girls' room and fix your top!"

TRECE
CHAPTER 13
MY WACKY MIXED-UP
SPANGLISH DAY!

"How about puppies?"

Later that morning in class, Sissy was reading animals off her list for our project. Our desks were pushed back into groups of three. We still didn't have a team list of animals to pick from. We spent too much time arguing yesterday.

I rolled my eyes. "Sissy, puppies are cute. But Mr. F said no farm animals or pets."

"I like pets," Sissy whined.

"I like slugs," Johnny said.

I shook my head and muttered, "You would."

Sissy and Johnny started fighting over another animal, but my head kept nodding. I was soooo sleepy. . . .

I shook my head, trying to wake up. I looked around.

In the back of the room, I spotted Melvin, the class iguana. An *un*common pet. And Mr. F did say it was okay to pick Melvin.

"*Una iguana.*" I pointed.

"Huh?" Johnny and Sissy turned to look.

"Like Melvin," I added quickly. "We could choose *una iguana.*"

Uh-oh, I thought, *I'm doing it again.*

At least "iguana" is the same in both languages.

"No way!" Billy Wong turned to us. "*We've* got Melvin! We already voted."

Jasmine, who was in Billy's group, shrugged. Then she crossed her eyes.

I crossed my eyes back and smiled.

"Fine," I said to Billy. "Keep Melvin. We'll think of something even better."

I checked my list again. Everything was crossed off.

"I'm fresh out of animals," I told them. "How about you?"

Sissy nodded. Johnny shrugged and tossed down his pencil. I could see everything was crossed off his list, too.

"Okay," I said, "why don't we start a new list? Let's just call off animals. Sissy, you write them down. We'll choose later."

"Hey! Who made you boss?" Sissy's face got all pink and crinkled up.

I sighed. I was too pooped to start arguing again so I said, "Okaaaay . . . I'll do it."

She picked up her pencil. "No, *I'll* do it.

Because *I* want to. Not because *you* told me to."

We started calling out animals, real fast. Sissy bent over her paper, trying to keep up.

"Worms!" From Johnny.

"Kittens!" From Sissy.

"*¡Un elefante!*" *Oops!* That was me.

"Rats!" Johnny.

"Goldfish!" Sissy.

"A *jirafa*!" *Uh-oh!* Me again.

"Bats!"

"Ponies!"

"A *tortuga!*" *Yikes!* "I mean a turtle."

While we called out animals, I watched Sissy. She was busily writing down everything we said. Her perfect blond curls jiggled as she wrote. She hadn't noticed my Spanish yet.

The words were too similar to English . . . so far.

I glanced at Johnny. He was staring at me. A wide smirk spread across his face.

"Hey!" he said. "As long as we're calling out animals in Spanish, why don't we choose — what was that word? Oh, yeah . . . *moscas*. The little bugs that *fly* around Maritza Pizza!"

My face got hot enough to fry *tostones* — deep-fried green bananas.

"*¡Caracoles!*" I stomped an angry foot and glared at him.

"What's going on?" Mr. F came over.

His eyebrows flew up high above his glasses. "Maritza, do I have to write another note to your parents?"

Mr. F peered down at me over his glasses.

My heart was racing faster than a hamster on an exercise wheel.

"*Por favor*, don't do that!" My cheeks sizzled.

Finally, Mr. F sighed. "All right, Martiza. But don't make me have to warn you again," he replied. Then he did a double take. "Maritza, are you practicing your Spanish today?"

Oops! I was hoping he wouldn't notice.

Now my ears began to burn. "Umm . . . Mr. Fine, I think I'm *un poco* — uh, a little — mixed-up today. I didn't get *mucho* sleep last night."

Someone snorted. "Maritza Pizza is fried. She got left in the oven too long."

I snapped my head around. It was Johnny Wiley — who else?

"John . . ." Mr. F warned.

"That's okay, Mr. Fine." I took a deep breath. I knew I needed to use my head . . . and hold my temper.

"He doesn't bother me. *No me molesta.* Umm . . . may I tell the *clase* something?"

"Is it important?"

"*Sí, señor* — uh . . . yes, sir — *muy importante.*"

I stood and faced the class. "From now

on, *me llamo* Gabi — that's short for Gabriela, my middle *nombre* — umm . . . name. So call me Gabi.

"*Mucha gente* . . . uh . . . lots of people use their middle *nombres* — even famous *gente* like Annie Oakley. Her real *nombre* was Phoebe Anne Oakley."

I glared at Johnny. "*Ahora* . . . uh, NOW there won't be any *more* Maritza or Maritza Pizza. *¡No más!*"

I stomped a spunky foot.

That's when Johnny burst out laughing.

"Oh, even better," he said. "We've got a new kid in the class — Blabby Gabby! It's the perfect name for such a blabbermouth!"

That's when I *really* lost it. I was so sure that when I changed my name, Johnny would stop pestering me. I couldn't believe he ruined my plan.

What good is using your head if your best plans get messed up?

My boots would have worked. Spunky feet always work!

"I'm going to *agarrarte*!" I yelled at Johnny that I was going to get him.

Then I yelled all sorts of things in a mix of

Spanish and English that I don't remember. But I DO remember doing a lot of spunky-feet stomping.

And I remember that Johnny and I BOTH got one hour of detention after school . . . together!

But I guess I'd mixed in enough English that Johnny got the point. During detention he sat as far from me as possible.

I sat in the front on the left side. He sat *waaaay* in the back — on the right.

If he'd been any closer to the wall, he would have been outside.

And more *importante,* I never heard a peep out of him.

CATORCE
CHAPTER 14
VOICES OF THE COQUÍ

¡Ay, ay, ay! What a crazy mixed-up day! I thought as I walked home from school after detention.

Spanish, English! English, Spanish! Spanglish! Spanglish!

I hoped I'd never have another two days at school like the last two. EVER!

When I finally got home, nobody was there.

Strange. *Someone* should be home. Mami and Papi never leave us kids alone.

I searched the kitchen for a note.

Nada. Nothing.

I would have gotten scared, but I was too

tired. I felt like a little kid who hasn't had her nap. Good thing it was almost Saturday. I could sleep in.

I went to my room and yanked on my boots. Tired as I was, I had to figure out how to deal with Johnny Wiley and how to stop losing my temper.

Maybe a snack would help me think . . . a snack and my boots.

As I passed the family room, enjoying the feel of my boots, I heard a shout in the backyard. I ran to the sliding glass door.

And you won't believe this! Abuelita was halfway up a tall oak tree. She was sitting on a branch!

"Abuelita!" I ran outside. "*¿Qué haces?*"

Abuelita grinned. "*Un pajarito* fell out of his nest. I put him back. Just in time, too. Tippy was about to pounce on him."

She swung her legs like Miguelito does when he's happy.

Tippy watched her from the bottom of

the tree. His tail flicked back and forth like it does when he's all huffy. Then he wandered off to sulk under a bush.

"Help me down, Gabrielita," said Abuelita. Move that chair over here for me."

I dragged the chair around to the other side of the tree. Abuelita slid down the trunk like she was my age.

I held my breath until she was safely down. "Mami would be very unhappy if she knew you were climbing trees again."

Abuelita jumped off the chair. She was all surprised — like she didn't know what I was talking about. "Tree? What tree?"

At the look on my face, she winked. "Come inside, Gabrielita. I have a snack for you."

Hand in hand, we skipped into the kitchen. "Where is everybody?" I asked.

"Your *tío* had some business to take care of. And your *mami* and *tití* took Miguelito to the mall. I wanted to stay and wait for you. So we could visit." Abuelita smiled and raised one eyebrow. "Quietly."

I remembered *el gallinero* this morning and giggled.

Abuelita took a plate from the fridge.

"Yumm!" I clapped and did my hop-skip-wiggle dance. "*¡Queso blanco y pasta de guayaba!* My favorite!" I *love* white cheese and guava paste!

"I know," she said. "I brought it fresh from Puerto Rico just for you kids."

I took giant steps to the table. My boots went *kathump*! *kathump*! *kathump*! on the tile floor!

That's when Abuelita noticed my feet. "Expecting trouble?"

I giggled. "Why does everyone think there's going to be trouble if I'm wearing my boots? Sometimes I just like wearing them. They help me think."

Abuelita smiled and sat next to me.

I kept saying, "Ummm ... umm ..." I swung my spunky feet like Miguelito.

When I was done, I licked my fingers. *"Gracias, Abuelita.* That was yummy."

"Oh?" She chuckled. "I couldn't tell."

Then she put her arm around me and held me close. I breathed in her lavender smell. Today it was mixed with a little garlic from cooking.

Mami can never stop Abuelita from cooking when we're together. Mami can't stop Abuelita from doing *anything* she wants to do. Even if it's something that's not very good for her — like climbing trees.

"I've missed you, Abuelita," I said. "I'm glad you came to visit."

She kissed me on the forehead. "I've missed you, too, Gabrielita. Very much. Maybe ... maybe I'll stay a little longer this time."

"Oh, Abuelita, really? *¡Qué chévere!*" I flung my arms around her neck. "That is SO cool! We're going to have SO much fun!"

Abuelita giggled — a really silly giggle. "*Sí, Gabrielita. Lots* of fun!"

For a moment I remembered how much Abuelita snored. I wouldn't be getting much sleep after all. But she'd only be sleeping with me two more nights. Tití Alicia was going home on Sunday.

Abuelita took a flat paper bag off the table. I was too busy eating to notice it before.

"Here, Gabrielita, I brought you a present from Puerto Rico. I thought it might remind you of the times you've visited me."

Inside the bag was a music tape. But when I took it out, it wasn't music at all. It had a picture of a *coquí* on the cover and was called, *Voces del Coquí. Voices of the Coquí.*

A *coquí* is a tiny tree frog that lives only in Puerto Rico. Its job is to sing *Co-KEE! Co-KEE! Co-KEE!* each night and when it rains. That's what you hear in Puerto Rico instead of crickets.

I sighed. Everyone has a job. Even the *co-*

quí. But I wasn't doing my job right. I couldn't seem to stop using my feet and start using my head.

I turned to Abuelita. She was grinning. "Now you can fall asleep to the sound of the *coquí* singing, not your Abuelita snoring."

I felt my cheeks get warm. She knew!

I looked back at the cover. I'd never seen the word *coquí* spelled out. I put my finger on the "i" with the accent on it.

Wouldn't it be cool to have a name with an accent in it?

Then — you'll never guess! — I came up with the perfect plan to stop Johnny from teasing me about my name.

"*¡Gracias, Abuelita!*"

We gave each other a great-big, super-*abuelita*-and-*nieta* hug.

For anyone who doesn't speak-a the lingo, that's a super-grandmother-and-granddaughter hug!

QUINCE
CHAPTER 15
GET READY FOR GABÍ!

"Class," Mr. Fine began on Monday morning, "Maritza — I mean, Gabi — has two things she would like to share with us. Gabi?"

Our desks were in their usual spots — in rows facing the front. We hadn't broken up into project groups yet.

I walked to the chalkboard and in great big letters, I wrote: GABÍ.

I turned to the class. "The first is that this is how you spell my name."

Jasmine grinned real big.

Devin tugged her hair.

On the board, I had put an extra big accent on the "i."

I pointed to it. "See this accent? It means that you say my name 'Ga-BEE.' Not 'GAB-bee.' And it does NOT rhyme with 'Blabby.'"

I looked at Johnny. His forehead was all crinkled, but he didn't say anything.

Devin gave her hair a double tug.

Jasmine crossed her eyes.

They both grinned.

I grinned back.

"The second thing is this tape." I held up the *coquí* tape.

First, I turned off the lights. Then I slipped the tape into Mr. F's boom box. I turned up the volume. Right away, the room was filled with tiny voices: *Co-KEE! Co-KEE! Co-KEE!*

The whole class gave a big gasp. Then they were so quiet, they seemed to be holding their breaths. It felt like we had stepped

into a rain forest . . . right in the mountains of Puerto Rico.

After a while, Sissy held up her hand.

"Sissy?" said Mr. Fine.

"What makes that pretty sound? A bird?"

Mr. Fine bowed and swished his arm at me. "Gabí?" He said it right — "Ga-BEE."

"No, that's what's so cool!" I said. "It's a tiny tree frog — half the size of my pinkie!"

I turned the lights back on and held up my little finger.

Everyone gasped again.

"You want to see a picture?" I held up the cover of the tape.

Everyone leaned forward in their desks.

"I can't see! I can't see!" they said.

Johnny raised his hand. "Mr. Fine, can I pass it around so everyone can see it?"

"*May* I," said Mr. F. Then he turned to me. "Gabí? Is that all right?"

"Oh . . . um . . ."

Johnny leaned way into his desk. He reminded me of a puppy waiting for a treat.

"Oh, okay," I said.

Johnny bounced to my side. He looked down at the picture of the tiny brown frog sitting inside a big red flower.

He sucked in his breath.

"Cool," he whispered. "Very cool."

I'd never stood so close to Johnny before.

And I'd never heard him whisper.

It made me listen — the way Mami had made me listen when I was little, just by whispering. And what I heard was someone who wasn't *all* nasty.

"Do you think we could do our animal project on the *coquí*?" he asked me.

My mouth fell open. "Uh . . . sure. But we have to ask Sissy."

Johnny took the picture to Sissy. "What do you think?"

Sissy stared at it for a long time. Then she whispered, too. I think she said, "Cool."

"Are you with us?" Johnny asked her. "Want to do our project on the *coquí*?"

"Yeah," she said. "That would be *way* cool." And she smiled at me.

Johnny took back the picture and stared at it again. "Hey! Look at this! The *coquí* spells its name the same way Gabí does. With an accent on the "i.""

And you won't believe what he said next!

"You even say it the same way. Ga-BEE. Co-KEE." He grinned. "Gabí the *coquí*!"

I slapped my forehead.

I looked at Devin. She was biting her lips together, trying not to laugh.

I looked at Jasmine. She squeezed her eyes shut and put her hand over her mouth.

I looked at Mr. Fine. His upper lip was twitching.

Suddenly, I started laughing. I laughed and I laughed and I laughed.

And the whole class laughed with me.

Everyone but Johnny. His mouth was hanging open.

Now I grinned. Real big. "If Gabí the *coquí* is all you can call me, that's okay. In fact, it's better than okay. I LIKE it!"

* * *

As I raced home after school, I sang to myself: *I did it! I did it! I DID IT!*

I spoiled my worst enemy's evil plans. And I did it with my head — not my spunky feet. So I never gave away my secret identity. Or got in trouble.

I ran inside and pulled on my boots.

My RED boots.

With the white moons and stars carved on the sides.

I stomped around my room.

I jumped on the bed. Boots and all.

"Watch out, world!" I yelled. "Bullies be warned! Get ready for Gabí!

"*¡Gabí está aquí!*"

¡HABLA ESPAÑOL!
(That means: *Speak Spanish!*)

abuelita (ah-booeh-LEE-tah): grandma

ají (ah-HEE): chili pepper

ajo (AH-hoh): garlic

alfombra (ahl-FOHM-brah): carpet, rug

almuerzo (ahl-MOOWEHR-soh): lunch

amor (ah-MOHR): love

bobo (BOH-boh): silly, foolish

botas (BOH-tahs): boots

cálmate (KAHL-mah-teh): calm down

¡Caracoles! (kah-rah-KOH-lehs): snails; can also be used to mean "Yikes!" or "Wow!" or "Doggone it!"

chévere (CHEH-behr-eh): Cool!

cocina (koh-SEE-nah): kitchen

coco (KOH-koh): coconut

comer (koh-MEHR): to eat

congelador (kohn-heh-lah-DOHR): freezer

contento (kohn-TEN-toh): happy

cuchichear (koo-chee-cheh-AHR): to whisper

dormir (dohr-MEER): to sleep

elefante (eh-leh-FAHN-teh): elephant

gente (HEN-teh): people

gracias (GRAH-seeyahs): thank you

guagua (GOOWAH-goowah): bus or van

hamburguesa (ahm-buhr-GEH-sah): hamburger

helado (eh-LAH-doh): ice cream

hija (EE-hah): daughter

importante (eem-pohr-TAN-teh): important

inglés (een-GLEHS): English

jirafa (hee-RAH-fah): giraffe

leche (LEH-cheh): milk

lo siento (loh SEEYEN-toh): I am sorry.

mala / malo (MAH-lah / MAH-loh): bad

¡mira! (MEE-rah): Look!

mosca (MOHS-kah): fly

muchacha (moo-CHAH-chah): girl

muchacho (moo-CHAH-cho): boy

muy bueno (moowee BOOEH-noh): very good

nada (NAH-dah): nothing

nieta (NEEYEH-tah): granddaughter

noche (NOH-cheh): night

nombre(s) (NOHM-breh(s)): name(s)

oreja (oh-REH-hah): ear

pajarito (pah-hah-REE-toh): little bird; baby bird

papas fritas (PAH-pahs FREE-tahs): french fries

perro (PEH-rroh): dog

picante (pee-KAN-teh): spicy hot

platos (PLAH-tohs): plates

por favor (pohr fah-VOHR): please

¿Qué? (KEH): What?

¿Qué haces? (KEH AH-sehs): What are you doing?

¿Qué pasa? (KEH PAH-sah): What's going on?; What's happening?; What's up?

Te quiero (teh KEEYEH-roh): I love you.

rabo (RAH-boh): tail

rana (RAH-nah): frog

rápido (RAH-pee-doh): quickly

roncar (rohn-KAHR): to snore

no sé (noh SEH): I don't know.

sí (SEE): yes

sorpresa (sohr-PREH-sah): surprise

tía (TEE-ah): aunt; **tío** (TEE-oh): uncle

tití (tee-TEE): auntie

tortilla de guineo (tohr-TEE-yah deh gee-NEH-oh): banana omelet

tortuga (tohr-TOO-gah): turtle; tortoise

#2 Who's That Girl?

I smiled as I peddled my bike down the sidewalk to the new neighbor's house.

Miguelito peddled beside me on his big blue plastic tricycle. It made a huge racket that I was trying to ignore.

Soon we reached the end of the block.

"*¡Mira! ¡Mira!*" Miguelito pointed to the big truck. "*¡El camión!*"

"*Shhh!* I see it. Remember what we said about being *quiet*?"

Miguelito put his pudgy finger on his lips. "Shhh, very *quiet*," he whispered.

The back doors of the truck were open. A big, old ramp ran down the back of the truck to the street.

Two huge men were carrying a couch down the ramp.

I glanced around. The front double doors of the house were open. But the house was dark inside. I couldn't see the new neighbors.

I looked for signs of kids. Lots of big boxes were stacked on the lawn. But no toys or bicycles . . .

"Careful, kids," one of the big men said. "Stay clear of the truck . . ."

"Are you the new neighbor?" I asked.

"Nah, kid. I'm just one of the movers. The new owners aren't here yet. Real estate lady let us in."

"Oh," I said. "When will they move in?"

"Not my business." He put down the box to wipe his face. He was all sweaty.

"Do they have kids?" Miguelito asked.

"You kids are full of questions, aren't you?"

Miguelito nodded. "There's lots we want to know."

The man laughed. "Yeah, kid. Me, too. Like sometimes I want to know what's the point?"

"Huh?" Miguelito and I said. Some grown-ups are really weird.

"Yeah, honey. *Huh?* That's what I say."

The man picked up the box and took it inside.

We waited another minute. When no one else came out of the house, I glanced around. No one was looking.

"Stay right here, Miguelito. Don't move."

I stepped to the back of the truck. I peeked inside.

Way in the back were three bicycles: two big boys' bikes and one small one.

And you won't believe this! The small one was just like mine.

But it was pink and purple.

A girl's bike!